6/11/2022

This book belongs to:

June

From Mimi

and

Grandpa Randy

MORE
5-Minute
PRINCESS
Stories

Written by Lara Bergen
Illustrated by the Disney Storybook Artists

Disney
PRESS

New York

Printed in the United States of America

ISBN 0-7868-3470-6

Library of Congress Catalog Card Number: 2003103008

Visit www.disneybooks.com

Contents

THE LITTLE MERMAID

Ariel's Big Rescue

The news was traveling rapidly throughout the undersea world—a human ship had been spotted up on the surface not too far away.

"Flounder," Ariel said excitedly to her best friend. "Come on! Let's go look at the ship. Maybe we'll see some humans!"

"Uh, Ariel," Flounder began, "I don't think it's a good idea. Your father—"

"No, Flounder, listen," Ariel replied. "Daddy will never find out. And as for the humans, they won't see us if we just pop our heads above water for a minute. It'll be fine, honest!"

Soon Ariel and Flounder were swimming close to a large schooner.

"Look at it, Flounder!" Ariel exclaimed. "It must be a royal ship! It's so big!"

"Yeah, now let's get out of here, Ariel!" Flounder said shakily.

Ariel was thrilled as she swam to the surface. Sailors scurried about on deck. A captain stood at the bow. And there was a girl . . . someone who looked just like a princess. Her braided black hair was gathered at the top of her head, with pearls laced through it, and she wore a beautiful red dress.

Suddenly, the ship lurched, causing everyone aboard to stumble and fall. The sailors began scrambling about and shouting. A few minutes later, the captain approached the girl.

"Princess, I'm afraid I have some bad news," Ariel heard him say. "Nothing to worry about, but our ship has hit a reef and sprung a leak. Now, we're close enough to shore that we can make it. But I'm afraid we will have to toss extra items overboard to lighten the load. That will include your baggage, of course. Terribly sorry."

"Don't be sorry, Captain," the princess replied. "I'll do anything I can to help."

Ariel and Flounder quickly ducked below the surface.

"Let's take a look at that leak," Ariel said. "Maybe we can help."

As the two friends went under the ship, they noticed that it was not merely a small leak. There was a large hole in the hull, and water was rushing into the ship! The captain must have been trying to protect the princess by not letting her know how serious it was.

"Quick, Flounder!" Ariel said. "Gather all the seaweed you can! We'll stuff it into the hole. Maybe it will slow the leak enough to give them time to get to shore!"

Soon Ariel and Flounder were plugging the hole with kelp. Then they swam next to the ship as it started moving toward land. Their plan was working!

"Woo-hoo!" cried Flounder when the ship finally reached the shore. "We did it! They're going to make it!"

Relieved, Ariel poked her head above the surface and took one last look at the ship. How Ariel wished she could talk with the princess, just for a moment, to find out what it was really like to be human!

"We'd better go now, Flounder," she said, sighing.

But when she started swimming toward home, she gasped. There, on the ocean floor, was a trunk, overflowing with honest-to-goodness, real human clothes. To Ariel, it was as good as a treasure chest!

"Flounder, this must be the princess's trunk!" she exclaimed. Hats, gloves, capes, corsets, jewelry—Ariel didn't know what they were called, but she tried on each and every one of them.

"Are you sure those holes are for your arms?" Flounder asked as Ariel struggled for a moment with a pair of frilly bloomers.

"Oh, yes, they must be!" She grinned. "They're so cute!"

Then Ariel pulled a long, blue gown out of the trunk. "I've never seen anything so beautiful!" she exclaimed.

Carefully, she held it up in front of her and smiled.

"Gee, Ariel, you look almost . . . human," Flounder said.

"I know." Ariel sighed. "Isn't it wonderful?"

Then she stopped. She thought of the human princess onshore, by now missing her lovely clothes and jewelry.

"You know, these things don't belong to me," Ariel said. "I should really return them to their rightful owner."

"Oh, no!" Flounder replied. "We're not going anywhere near those humans."

But that night, with Flounder by her side, Ariel took the trunk close enough to shore so that the tide could wash it up on the beach. Playing dress-up had been fun, but it felt much better to return the items to the princess.

"Maybe someday I'll be able to walk onshore and wear dresses just like hers," Ariel said dreamily. "I'll be a human princess, too—"

"Yeah, right," Flounder said. "And I'll be your king. Now, come on. Let's go home before we get into any more trouble!"

Aladdin

A Magical Surprise

*I*t was a lovely day in Agrabah. The sun was shining brightly, with the gentlest of breezes drifting through the air. And in the garden of the palace, Princess Jasmine was pouring a bowl of tea for her pet Bengal tiger, Rajah.

It was, in fact, just like every other lovely day in Agrabah—and that was just the problem.

"Sorry to be so glum," Jasmine said to Rajah. "It's just that I was hoping to spend some time with Aladdin, but I can't seem to find him anywhere."

Rajah nodded his great, furry head sympathetically.

"To tell you the truth," Jasmine went on, "I'll bet Aladdin went off on the Magic Carpet today and completely forgot about me!"

Just then, to Jasmine's surprise, the Magic Carpet zoomed into the garden and stopped right in front of her—all alone. Jasmine watched it dart about and wave its tasseled corners, as if it were trying to tell her something. Clearly, Aladdin wasn't spending his day with the Magic Carpet!

15

"Whatever's wrong?" Jasmine asked it. "Where's Aladdin, Magic Carpet?" But when the Magic Carpet did a quick flip, Jasmine realized it wanted her to jump aboard for a ride. The Magic Carpet eagerly swooped down to pick her up, and soon Jasmine was riding high above land.

"Oh, Magic Carpet, it's beautiful up here," Jasmine said with a sigh. "But I'm worried about Aladdin."

Jasmine's thoughts began racing.

I hope Jafar hasn't somehow returned and locked him up! Or what if Aladdin's hurt himself and can't get help? she wondered.

"Magic Carpet, can you take me to Aladdin?" Jasmine asked. But the Magic Carpet didn't respond. Did the Magic Carpet not know where Aladdin was?

Taking matters into her own hands, Jasmine urged the Magic Carpet on a search for Aladdin, riding over the desert, the marketplace, everywhere she could think of. Yet, nearly an hour later, they still had not found Aladdin.

At last, the princess told the Magic Carpet to return to the palace. Perhaps there they could get some more help.

Before long, the Magic Carpet landed with a bump right in the middle of the castle garden.

"SURPRISE!"

As Jasmine stood, dumbfounded, dozens of her friends and family leaped out from behind the bushes, carrying presents.

Delighted, Jasmine clapped her hands and smiled from ear to ear. But what was this all about? It wasn't her birthday—or any other special holiday for that matter.

Suddenly, Aladdin popped out from behind a large cake.

"Happy anniversary, Jasmine!" he said, beaming. "Are you surprised?"

"Surprised?" Jasmine replied. "Of course I am!" Then she added to Aladdin with a whisper, "It's not our anniversary!"

Aladdin smiled and whispered back, "It's the anniversary of the day we first met in the marketplace. I thought it was cause for a celebration."

Jasmine smiled and kissed Aladdin on the cheek. But when she looked at the Magic Carpet, she stopped abruptly. "Why, you sneaky thing!" she said. Then she smiled. "You were in on this surprise all along, weren't you?" She ruffled the Magic Carpet's tassles. Then she leaned in to whisper to it.

In an instant, the Magic Carpet
swooped Aladdin and Jasmine playfully up into the air
and gave them a wild ride over the entire garden!

"Whoa!" cried Aladdin.

"Keep it up, Magic Carpet!" Jasmine shouted, laughing. Then she turned to Aladdin.
"This is what you get for scaring me like that."

"Hey, I'm sorry," Aladdin said. "I didn't mean to worry you. . . ."

"It's okay," she said with a smile. "This party, my friends and family—it's all wonderful."
This would certainly be a day she would never forget.

21

Snow White
and the Seven Dwarfs
A Royal Visit

Snow White was just about as happy as a princess could be. She lived in a beautiful castle—with a handsome and loving prince. She didn't have to worry about her wicked stepmother anymore. But, alas, she did miss one thing. . . .

"I've just been thinking about the Dwarfs," she said one day to the Prince. "It's been too long since I've seen them."

"Well, why don't we go pay them a visit?" the Prince suggested. "Their cottage is not so very far away."

Snow White's face instantly lit up. "But of course!" she said. "Let's go today!"

Sleepy was just waking up when a bluebird landed on the Dwarfs' windowsill.

"Say, there's a boat in his nose. Er—a note in his toes," said Doc, noticing the envelope in the bird's claws.

"Looks like, uh . . . uh . . . ah . . . ah-*choo* . . . letter," said Sneezy.

"Indeed," said Doc. "But who would have sent it?"

Then he reached for the envelope, and the scent of sweet perfume drifted his way.

"Why, it's from Snow White!" Doc exclaimed.

"Achoo!" Sneezy sneezed.

"Well, stop sniffin' the durn thing and read it already," grumbled Grumpy.

"A-hem," Doc cleared his throat as the other Dwarfs eagerly waited.

"'My dear Dwarfs,'" Doc began. "Heh-heh, she calls us 'dear'!"

"Oh, get on with it," said Grumpy.

Doc scanned the note. "Well, um . . . well, golly gee! She's comin' for a visit! Today!" he cried. "At noon!"

"Hooray!" Happy cheered. "Snow White is coming!"

But the other six Dwarfs looked around their untidy cottage—at their unmade beds, their wrinkled clothes, and their dirty dishes piled high in the sink.

"She's comin' *today*?" Bashful gulped. "But we can't let her see the place lookin' like this!"

"And she's comin' at *noon*!" Grumpy huffed. "You know what that means, don'tcha? She'll want lunch. Someone's gonna have to cook!"

"Mmnnn . . . I'll need a nap," Sleepy said with a yawn.

"No naps and no more talkin'," Doc announced as he grabbed a broom. He handed it to Dopey. "We have a lot to do, men! Sleepy, you bake—er, *make* the beds. Bashful, you fold the clothes. Sneezy, you dust the furniture. Dopey will sweep the doors—er, *floors*. And Happy and Grumpy and I will fix somethin' suitable for Snow White to eat. Now, off to work we go! Go! Go!"

The Dwarfs started right away. But cooking and cleaning were not their strong points. Sleepy lay down in the middle of Grumpy's bed. Bashful hid behind a pile of clothes. Sneezy sneezed dust all around the room. And Dopey kept knocking things over with his broom.

As for Happy and Grumpy, they began to argue over what kind of sandwiches to make.

"Snow White likes peanut butter and jelly, I know," Happy declared.

"She likes ham and cheese," Grumpy grumbled.

By the time Doc finally got them to agree on something, the clock struck twelve and there was a soft rap upon the door.

"They're . . . ahh . . . ahh . . . *heeere*!" Sneezy sneezed. "Wake up, Sleepy!"

All at once, the Dwarfs ran up to open the door for their beloved princess, and they smiled as she hugged each and every one of them, then kissed them all on their foreheads.

"How I've missed you all!" she cried.

"Please, forgive the mess, Princess," Bashful whispered to her.

"Oh, Bashful," Snow White said with a laugh. "You must forgive *me* for giving you such short notice! Besides, I've come to see *you*—not your cottage."

"Would you care for a ham and jelly sandwich?" Doc offered. "Or peanut butter and cheese?"

"Oh, how sweet," Snow White kindly replied. "If I had known you'd go to all this trouble, I wouldn't have brought a picnic of my own."

"Picnic!" the Dwarfs exclaimed.

Just then, the Prince walked in with an overflowing basket.

"What's in it?" Doc asked hopefully.

"Oh, just some roast chicken and deviled eggs. Cinnamon bread and butter. Corn and tomatoes from the royal garden. Sugar cookies and a fresh apple pie . . . but let's eat your sandwiches first," said Snow White.

The Dwarfs looked at one another, and Doc cleared his throat.

"Nonsense, Princess," he told Snow White. "We can have ham and jelly any time. Let's enjoy the food you've brought. And you can tell us all about living happily after."

And that's exactly what they did.

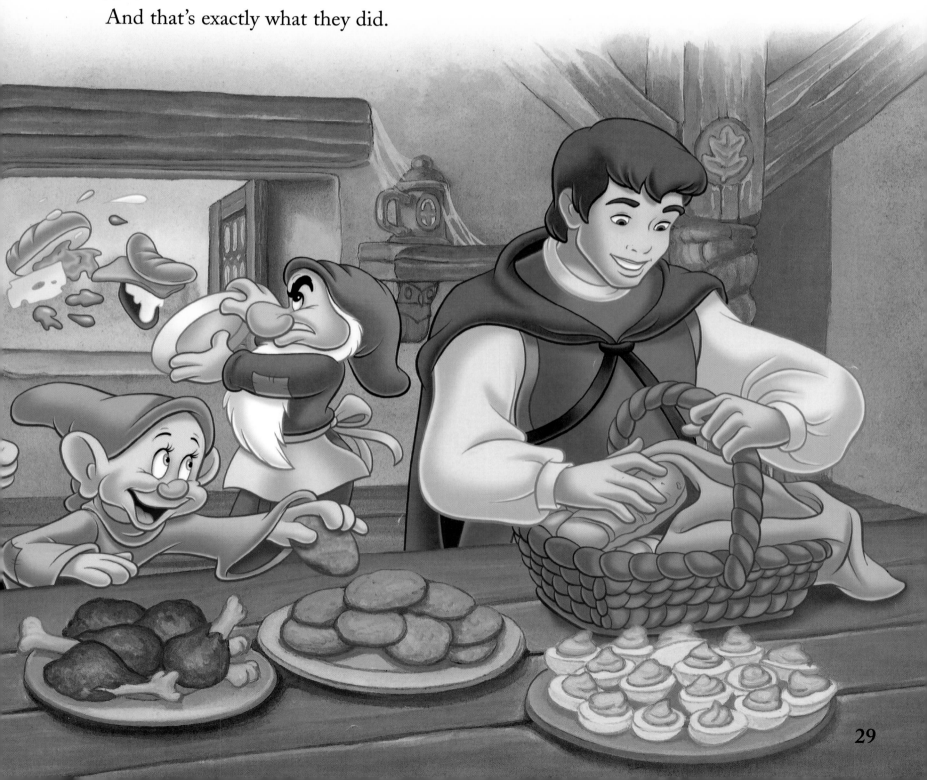

Sleeping Beauty
The Wedding Gift

Sleeping Beauty had received True Love's Kiss at last. And now she was living happily back at the castle with her parents, preparing for the wonderful day she would marry the man of her dreams, Prince Phillip.

Naturally, the whole castle was abuzz. The royal gardeners were gathering the most fragrant flowers from the palace garden. The royal chefs were cooking up the grandest of wedding banquets. And the royal bakers were assembling a wedding cake tall enough to feed the entire kingdom.

And then there was the royal dressmaker, who, with her staff of twenty-two, had the most honored job of all—sewing the wedding dress of Princess Aurora's dreams.

The dressmaker curtsied to Aurora, her parents, and the three good fairies who had cared for Aurora for sixteen years.

"If you please, Your Royal Highness, what did you have in mind?" the dressmaker politely asked Aurora, as she held up samples to show the princess.

"Well," Aurora began, "I—"

"You'll want white, of course," the dressmaker broke in, "though not too white. I see something more vanilla, to complement your lovely skin." She motioned to her assistants. "As Your Highness will see, I have some gorgeous ivory satin here. And an off-white brocade that's simply divine. Ah, yes!"

"Actually," Aurora said, "I—"

But the dressmaker wasn't done yet. "And by all means, you'll want a train! Twenty feet or so, I should say."

Truthfully, that wasn't what Aurora had had in mind at all. But before Aurora could say anything, the fairy Merryweather spoke up.

"But what if Briar Rose—oh, goodness me! I mean, Princess Aurora—doesn't want a dress that color?" she said, pointing to one of the samples.

Aurora smiled.

"What the dear girl needs is something *blue*," Merryweather said.

"Oh, no!" Flora scolded. "A wedding dress shouldn't be blue. It should be pink!"

Poor Aurora shook her head as she watched the fairies change the dress color.

"Or perhaps—" Fauna began.

"Just a minute now!" King Stefan declared, holding up his hand. "Pink, blue, ivory, or cream—I hereby decree that the color of the gown be left up to the bride."

Aurora sighed with relief and smiled as her father gave her shoulder a little squeeze.

Then the king went on. "The most important thing is that the dress be covered with *jewels*. Lots of them! After all, she *is* a princess!"

"Why, of course, Your Supreme Highness," the dressmaker said with a most reverent bow. "Lots of jewels. My thoughts exactly."

Aurora's face, once hopeful, suddenly fell. Jewels? Oh, dear. Wasn't that a little much?

While her father and the dressmaker discussed various bejeweled designs, Princess Aurora tried to think of the best way to tell them what kind of dress she herself wanted.

Then, suddenly, she felt a soft hand take hold of hers.

"Come, darling," her mother whispered, smiling. "I have something I'd like to show you." She nodded toward the king and dressmaker, deep in discussion. "I don't think they'll miss us for a few moments, do you?"

Together, the two walked up the stairs and into the Queen's dressing room. And there, Aurora watched her mother go to an old trunk, open it, and pull out a long, beautiful gown, edged with delicate lace and tiny pearls.

"This was my wedding dress when I was a princess," the Queen explained. "And my mother's before me. I had hoped one day you'd wear it—if you'd like to, of course."

"Oh, Mother!" Aurora exclaimed. "It's just what I had in mind!"

Moments later, Aurora went back downstairs, wearing her mother's wedding gown.

"Oohh!" The fairies gasped.

"Ahh!" The dressmaker sighed.

"Perfect!" declared her father.

One and all agreed that the dress looked as if it had been made especially for Aurora—and, in a very special way, it had been.

Beauty and the Beast
Belle's Special Treat

"'And from that moment on, the princess had flowers every day of her life. The End,'" Belle read and closed the book with a sigh.

"What a treat!" she said to the Beast, as she gazed out of his library window at the cold, snowy hills. "The winter is lovely, of course . . . but to have flowers every day, I'd give anything. Wouldn't you?"

The Beast looked surprised. He had no idea Belle loved flowers that much. He had had so much else on his mind, after all. But he had also never seen this longing look in Belle's eyes. And the amazing thing was, he knew he could do something about it!

That evening, after Belle had gone to sleep, the Beast made his way to a part of his castle he hadn't visited in years—the royal greenhouse.

"Are we really going where I think we're going?" Lumiere the candelabrum asked with delight, as he lit the Beast's way.

But his master only nodded. All of a sudden, the Beast was worried. What if the flowers he'd once taken such pride in (*too* much pride, many had said) had died over time, from loneliness and neglect? They were, after all, rare and delicate species, collected from almost every corner of the world. And the Beast hadn't laid eyes on them since the day the enchantress had cast her spell on him and his castle. He just hadn't seen the point of caring for silly flowers—when no one would be coming to compliment them anymore.

What shape would they be in? he wondered.

Fortunately, the gardener (who was now a trowel) and his two assistants

(transformed into a pair of clippers and a watering can, respectively) had watched over the greenhouse as best they could over the years. When the Beast walked in, he was pleased to see that his beloved flowers were still alive.

"There's still a lot of work to be done," he told Lumiere excitedly as he rolled up his sleeves and settled in to start working. But he knew he would enjoy every moment. And he did! He dug in the dirt, trimmed all sorts of plants, and pulled weeds. He tended his garden every day until it was back to its former glory.

One morning when Belle woke up, the first thing she saw was a big bouquet of daffodils—the earliest flowers of spring. "But it's still snowing outside," she said, utterly bewildered. "Wherever did these come from?"

Mrs. Potts just smiled. "Have a cup of tea, love," she said.

But Belle noticed that the Wardrobe, Mrs. Potts, and Chip were all smiling from ear to ear. Did they know something she didn't?

Throughout the day, Belle discovered flowers all over the castle. There were tulips in the dining room, lilies in the library, and six different colors of roses in the ballroom!

Finally, just as the sun was setting, Belle heard a knock on her door.

It was the Beast.

"Where have you been?" Belle asked. "I missed you."

"Really?" The Beast looked surprised.

"Really," Belle assured him. "And you've missed the most—"

Just then, Belle noticed there were leaves caught in the Beast's thick fur.

"Why, the flowers are from *you*!" she exclaimed.

"Oh, um . . ." the Beast answered gruffly. Then he added, "There's something I'd like to show you . . . that is, if you're willing."

"Of course," Belle said with a smile.

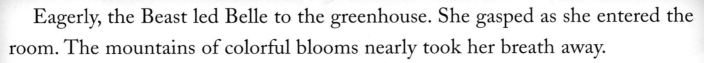

Eagerly, the Beast led Belle to the greenhouse. She gasped as she entered the room. The mountains of colorful blooms nearly took her breath away.

"I'd almost forgotten about this place," the Beast confessed. "That is, until you reminded me. Then I realized there *was* a way to have flowers every day."

"I really don't know how to thank you," Belle said, still amazed.

"Just enjoy them," the Beast told her. "If I'm not mistaken . . . that's what friends—and flowers—are for."